HUDSON
AND
TALLULAH
TAKE SIDES

by **Anna Kang**

illustrated by **Christopher Weyant**

two lions

To all our neighbors
for enriching our lives,
including Tank, Zoe, Zoey,
Finn, Mookie, Artemis, and Cleo.
Sometimes Hudson may not get along,
but he's always on your side.

Hudson!
Yay! Hudson's here!

Why would anyone want a dog for a friend?

Come on!
The mud is fine!

The mud is filthy.

That's the dude
who attacks my house!
Every day! At noon!

SPLASH!